The Christmas Bird

WRITTEN AND ILLUSTRATED BY

Bernadette Watts

NORTH-SOUTH BOOKS / NEW YORK / LONDON

ONE WINTER LONG AGO, the snow fell so deeply and for so long that all the world was frozen white and summer was almost forgotten.

On one cold night that snowy winter, as Katya helped her mother set the table, she told her about the strangers she had seen that day. "When I took the eggs to the innkeeper this morning," said Katya, "I saw a man and a woman at the door. They looked very tired."

"The innkeeper told me about them," said Katya's father. "There is no room at the inn, but he let them stay in a stable. At least they have hay there and some animals to keep them warm."

"Poor things," said Mother. "It's terrible to have to travel in this bitter-cold weather."

After Katya had gone up to bed, she heard footsteps crunching in the snow outside the house, and her father opening the door.

Katya crept to the window. Below, she saw shepherds standing in the light from the doorway.

"Where are you going?" she heard her father ask.

"You see that bright star high up in the sky?" said one of the shepherds. "Angels have told us that the star will lead us to a newborn King, so we are following it to find Him and give Him these lambs."

Katya looked up at the dark sky. High above, right over the distant stable, shone a brilliant star, one she had never seen before.

It took Katya a long time to fall asleep that night. As she drifted off, she thought, "I want to take the baby King a gift too."

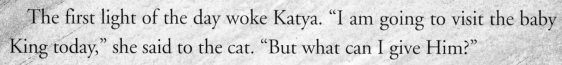

The first light of the day woke Katya. "I am going to visit the baby King today," she said to the cat. "But what can I give Him?"

Katya did not have many toys, but she had one she really loved, a wooden bird whistle. "I will give Him this," she said. "I am sure He will like it. And I will take you to see Him too," she told the cat. "The baby King will surely enjoy playing with you."

Her mother was baking when she came downstairs.

"I am going to visit the baby King," said Katya. "May I take some bread with me for His parents?"

Her mother gave her a piece of bread, and said, "Put on your warm boots. The snow is very deep."

Katya left the house with her arms full of the cat, the bread, and the wooden bird whistle.

She went through the village. But the cat did not like being carried away from his warm house. He twisted, kicked, and suddenly sprang out of Katya's arms, racing all the way back to his own door.

Katya was sorry not to have the cat for the baby King to play with. "But I still have a gift for Him," she said, "and bread for His parents."

She crossed the bridge over the frozen stream, leading away from the village toward the higher slopes.

She slowly trudged on as the ground rose sharply.

A reindeer appeared from among the trees, and came right up to her. It looked very hungry. "This is a big piece of bread," Katya thought. "I can give away a few crumbs. There will still be enough."

While she broke off bits of bread for the hungry reindeer, other small animals gathered around her. Katya gave them some bread too, and ate some herself. Soon all the bread was gone and Katya felt a little guilty. "At least I still have my bird to give Him," she told herself, "and that is the best gift of all."

The sky now darkened with the heavily falling snow. Katya's toes and fingers and nose tingled with cold as she climbed up the steep meadow. Then suddenly she stumbled, and as she fell, she dropped the bird.

Katya scraped wildly at the snow, tears stinging her cheeks. She jumped up and down to warm herself, then dug again.

At last her fingers touched the wooden bird! She brushed the snow off the whistle and blew it. But there was no sound. She blew again, harder, but still the bird was silent.

"Now I have nothing for the baby King," Katya said sadly, and turned to go home.

Then she saw the light from the stable door spreading like a path down to where she stood. She was tired, the last part of the meadow was the steepest, but step by step, clutching her bird, she came at last to the stable door.

The man and the woman inside smiled kindly at Katya. The Baby laughed and stretched out His tiny hands as if to welcome her.

Katya came in shyly. The cat was gone, the bread was gone, the song of the bird was gone.

But Katya knew only joy as she knelt close to the baby King and offered Him her broken gift.

The baby King closed His hands over the wooden bird. When He opened them again, a living bird flew up, whistling a beautiful song!

When Katya left the stable, the bird flew with her, singing cheerily. It followed her all the way home, and the journey did not seem long at all.

At home the bird perched on Katya's windowsill and sang to her, so that all her days were filled with joy.

First published in the United States, Great Britain, Canada,
Australia, and New Zealand in 1996 by North-South Books,
an imprint of Nord-Süd Verlag AG, Gossau Zürich, Switzerland.

Distributed in the United States by North-South Books Inc., New York.

Library of Congress Cataloging-in-Publication Data is available.
A CIP catalogue record for this book is available from The British Library.
ISBN 1-55858-603-2 (TRADE BINDING)
1 3 5 7 9 TB 10 8 6 4 2
ISBN 1-55858-604-0 (LIBRARY BINDING)
1 3 5 7 9 LB 10 8 6 4 2
Printed in Belgium

*For information about this and other North-South books,
visit our web site at:* http://www.northsouth.com